Austin asked Daddy, "Why do we put up lights at Christmas time?" He answered, "They are to remind us of the Town of Bethlehem where the first Christmas took place when Jesus was born." How many parents nowadays are able to provide such clear answer to their children? We must teach our children the true meaning of Christmas!

– Dr. Isao Ebihara, PhD, Author

Through imagination and a few fun-filled family traditions, Mr. Nobody continues to amuse and guide us through some of life's most valuable lessons. This festive collage of spirit-filled adventures will no doubt delight your whole family!

– Shona Durrant, Legal Assistant & Best Friend of 30 years!

MR. NOBODY'S

Christmas Treasury

Written by Diane Welch   Illustrated by Dave Welch

Mr. Nobody's Christmas Treasury

ISBN: 978-1-4866-0572-9

Word Alive Press
131 Cordite Road, Winnipeg, MB R3W 1S1
www.wordalivepress.ca

WORD ALIVE
—PRESS—

Cataloguing in Publication information may be obtained through Library and Archives Canada

This book is dedicated to my parents, Don and Lorraine Baycroft, for all the wonderful childhood memories created at Christmas time; as well as John and Marilynn Welch for creating wonderful Christmas traditions that have been passed on to our family through my amazing husband, Dave!

For the Love of our Dear Saviour, Jesus!

Merry Christmas!

Diane Welch
Author of *Introducing Mr. Nobody!*
and *Mr. Nobody's Shenanigans!*

The book you are about to read comes after *Introducing Mr. Nobody!* and *Mr. Nobody's Shenanigans!*

In a little yellow house on Maple Street live seven people: Mommy, Daddy, Katie, Hope, Page, Mr. Nobody, and me! My name is Austin, and I'll tell you lots of wonderful stories about Mr. Nobody and my family. We have a new family member now that you can read about in this book! You'll also hear about Zeus, our dog, who is good friends with Mr. Nobody.

A few things you should know about Mr. Nobody: he stands seven feet tall and three feet wide. He has thick long brown fur all over him and a cute little black nose. Mr. Nobody sleeps in an invisible bed in my room and can go invisible when he's scared or in one of his mischievous moods. He is kind, obedient, gentle and loves hugs, chocolates, coffee, and strawberry jam sandwiches and toast.

His favorite holiday is April Fools' Day, because he enjoys playing practical jokes and likes to bake Rock Apple Pie! He's fantastic at hiding shoes, hats, and mitts, but most of all he loves to hide Daddy's coffee because Daddy can't put his brain into imagination mode. Daddy can feel Mr. Nobody's weight, see coffee cups or items Mr. Nobody has baked, but can't see him doing things like sliding. But Daddy can sure feel the effects of Mr. Nobody's shenanigans!

So put your brain into imagination mode, and grab a cup of coffee or a cup of hot chocolate and come curl up with Mr. Nobody!

With love from all of us here at the little yellow house on Maple Street.

Mr. Nobody and the Twinkling Christmas Lights

In a little yellow house on Maple Street live seven people: Mommy, Daddy, Katie, Hope, Page, Austin, and Mr. Nobody!

It was a busy little yellow house, because it was Christmas.

The four of us kids were so excited about the chance of snow, presents, Christmas baking, shopping for gifts and tree decorating. You name it, we kids loved getting ready for Christmas!

It was a Saturday morning and the air outside was cold and crisp. Mr. Nobody was sitting at the kitchen table having his favorite breakfast: strawberry jam on toast and a delicious cup of hot coffee.

Mr. Nobody heard a weird sound: *Scritch, Scratch, Scritch, Twist, Twist, Crunch, Scritch*. What on earth was that sound? Where was that sound coming from?

Mr. Nobody ran out the front door and suddenly I heard *Clang, Clang, Kling, Bang*. "Help me!" screeched Mr. Nobody.

"What on earth?" I raced to the front door to where I heard the noise coming from and discovered Mr. Nobody wrestling with our huge steel ladder!

"Where did the ladder came from?" I asked Mr. Nobody.

"I don't know, it was in front of the door!" Mr. Nobody shrieked. Mr. Nobody was very shocked that he had somehow tangled himself right into our steel ladder!

I whirled around to see that Daddy was putting the lights on top of the roof. "Quick, let's put the ladder back on the front steps before Daddy needs the ladder to get off the roof."

Mr. Nobody noticed that Daddy was up on top of the roof putting up the reindeer set. Daddy hadn't heard or seen any of the commotion. Mr. Nobody and I got the ladder back into place. Good thing Daddy looked before he took a step down onto the ladder.

"Why do you put lights up at Christmas time?" Mr. Nobody wondered.

"Let's ask Daddy!"

Mr. Nobody and I went to see Daddy plug in the last of the lights.

"Hey buddy, I could sure use some coffee to warm me up! Brrr! It is starting to get cold out." Daddy shivered. So off Mr. Nobody, Daddy, and I went to have coffee and a hot cocoa for me.

"Daddy, why do we put up lights at Christmas time?"

Daddy took a sip of his coffee. "They are to remind us of the Town of Bethlehem where the first Christmas took place when Jesus was born."

"When can we open our presents?" asked Mr. Nobody.

Since Daddy didn't hear Mr. Nobody's question, I asked Daddy the same question only to see Daddy yawn and stretch and get up to head for the couch.

"Soon enough, Austin, soon enough. Why don't you and Mr. Nobody go check out the lights I put up?"

So I called Mommy and all three of the girls. "Let's go and check out the Christmas Lights!" I chimed.

Mommy and the girls put on their coats and we even got Zeus into his doggie jacket. Then we all went out to the crisp winter air. Daddy had worked all day putting up the lighted reindeer on the roof and lights in the maple tree and on the white picket fence. Colorful lights were placed around the doors and windows, too.

"What a beautiful sight! Wow! They are amazing!" Page exclaimed.

Katie and Hope ran into the house to get Dad to come see the lights, too! "Dad, come see... hey, you're sleeping!" Katie and Hope quietly replied.

Mr. Nobody placed his own favorite blue fuzzy blanket on top of Daddy and quietly whispered, "Thanks Daddy, for reminding us of the first Christmas in Bethlehem!"

It was a busy day in the little yellow house. Stay tuned for more Christmas adventures!

Love,

Austin

A Day in the Snow!

In a little yellow house all cosy and warm, we lay all asleep deep in dream world.

Mr. Nobody opened his big brown eyes and blinked away the sand from his sleepy eyes!

He yawned and stretched and squirmed down under the cosy blue blanket, and then Zeus our dog shoved his cold little black nose right into Mr. Nobody's big black nose.

Mr. Nobody knew that Zeus had to go outside. Reluctantly, Mr. Nobody placed his big furry feet on the cold floor and sauntered off to the front door with Zeus anxiously skipping along beside him.

Opening the door, Mr. Nobody got blasted with icy, cold, wintery air. There was one foot of snow outside. "Wow!" Mr. Nobody shouted. "Get up, get up, it snowed!" Mr. Nobody was so excited, he forgot to shut the front door!

Mr. Nobody ran to our room and yanked the covers off my bed. Then he couldn't resist tickling my bare feet that were sticking up in the frigid air.

Down Mr. Nobody ran to yank Katie's covers off her bed. Katie, murmured. "What! What happened?"

"It Snowed!"

You should have seen how quickly Katie sat up. "Snow, I love snow! And because we live in the lower mainland, it means no school!"

"Yeah!" Page and Hope yelled.

"Let's check out the computer first to see if there is a message from the school yet."

Brring! went the phone. Mommy slowly got out of bed. "Why is it so cold in this house?

Brring!

"I'm coming!" Mommy said.

Mr. Nobody ran into the kitchen to make his favorite drink, coffee, and put on some toast. Then he felt a chill, and realized he'd forgotten to close the front door! Mr. Nobody hurried to the door and shut it, stopping winter from getting inside the little yellow house.

Brring! went the phone.

"Hello?" Mommy sleepily replied.

"This is a message from your local school board. Due to snowfall overnight, there will be no school for today. Enjoy a snow day!"

Now let me explain. In other parts of Canada, snow is expected. Here where we live... yeah, not so much!

Mommy calmly sighed. "Snow day, Austin."

 Daddy got up to see three blue mugs of warm coffee on the kitchen table. "Wow! Mr. Nobody must be up, coffee is on!"

Daddy almost dropped his coffee. Standing in front of him was a little white snow clump with a funny looking brown tail sticking up in the air! Sure enough, when Zeus shook, off went all the snow all over the living room floor and Kitty too.

Kitty was not impressed with Zeus, let alone all this white stuff. While Mommy dried off Zeus and Kitty, Daddy went and called into work only to find out that there was no work for him as there was a power outage and too much snow.

"I better make sure we have plenty of batteries and candles in case we have a power outage here at home."

"Good thinking, Daddy," Mr. Nobody replied. But Daddy didn't hear Mr. Nobody's comment.

We four kids sat down to a bowl of steamy oatmeal, hot, creamy cocoa, and toast with mouth-watering strawberry jam!

After breakfast we all got out our sleds, warm coats, ski pants, and warm knitted hats.

Where on earth were our boots and mittens?

"Mr. Nobody, where did you hide our boots and mittens!" I called.

"If we can't find them, then no one plays outside. Even you, Mr. Nobody!" Mommy firmly stated.

Mr. Nobody went over to a big brown box high on a shelf and pulled the box down. In the brown box was all of our winter boots.

"Mr. Nobody, why did you do this?" Mommy asked.

"I was trying to help Mommy clean up the garage a bit, and then it was so tempting to just put the boots into this box and not tell Mommy where the boots were. Not so smart, if she is not going to let us go outside to play without them."

On went all the boots.

"Now where are our mittens?" we chimed.

Mr. Nobody went over to where Kitty was curled up on his special bed and pulled out the mittens hidden underneath the flannel blankets. Kitty again was not impressed!

"I put the mittens here to help keep Kitty warm and to plump up Kitty's bed a little, too," Mr. Nobody said quietly while patting Kitty.

"Well, very nice of you to think of Kitty. Now you can go and play outside," Mommy exclaimed.

Mommy pulled Austin on the blue sled, Daddy pulled Page and Hope on the long wooden sled, and Katie pulled Mr. Nobody on the green sled, all the way to the ski hill.

Mr. Nobody tried to snowboard on Page's board, but he kept doing bum drops and belly flops!

On and on, up and down the hill we went until we were very tired and cold. Hope looked around and asked, "Where is Mr. Nobody?"

We looked all over the hill and called, "Mr. Nobody, where are you?" Then I discovered a snowman beside a little Christmas tree. The snowman had big feet, a round belly, and a huge head and guess what? The snowman's big brown eyes were moving! Back and forth, back and forth. Can you believe it?

"Woah, come check out the snowman," I told Page, Mommy, and Hope.

"What on earth?"

"How is the snow man's eyes moving?"

"BOO!" shouted Mr. Nobody. Out of the snowman jumped Mr. Nobody!

We nearly jumped out of our skin. We all laughed and yelled. We couldn't believe the funny shenanigans Mr. Nobody played on us. Hope ran over to Daddy and Katie to tell them what had happened.

Mr. Nobody had snow on him and was starting to shiver quite a bit. Mommy wrapped his warm blue fuzzy blanket around Mr. Nobody and had him sit on the big wooden sled. Mr. Nobody was happy Mommy cared for him.

We gathered all of our sleds and started to head home for lunch. When Daddy went to pull the big sled that he thought was empty, he fell right down into the snow bank—KERPLUNK!!!

"What? Why is the sled so heavy?" shouted Daddy.

"Shhh, look!" I whispered.

Mr. Nobody was curled up in his blue fuzzy blanket, fast asleep. Poor Daddy said, "I can't see him but, I can sure feel him!"

"He is one heavy tired monster," puffed Katie as she helped Daddy pull Mr. Nobody all the way home.

It was a fantastic day at the ski hill. Remember to play safe, and have fun with your family this Christmas and all year long.

See you for more Christmas adventures at the little yellow house.

Love,

Austin

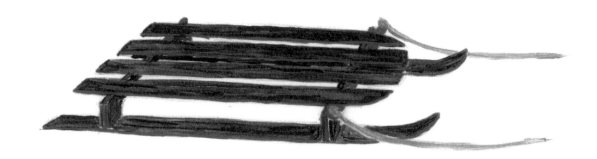

Mr. Nobody and the Fresh New Christmas Tree!

It was a busy day at our little yellow house on Maple Street. Mommy had mailed all the Christmas cards. She was lucky she got to mail *any* after Mr. Nobody discovered them. What do you think he did with the Christmas cards?

First, he started cutting out all the glittering pictures on the cards because he thought they would be pretty strung up on the Christmas tree. Mr. Nobody did a whole box of them before Mom discovered the mess. She had to go back to the store to buy a new box of cards!

Secondly, Mr. Nobody decided that the envelopes would make cool looking airplanes. He took the box of envelopes and ran his big claw under the edges and unstuck the glue, then he laid them flat and pressed on them with his furry paw. Very quickly, he folded every corner and then put a hole in the wing of the plane and tied a ribbon on it.

Mommy watched in disgust at all the mess all over my room and sighed. "Mr. Nobody, what are you doing now?"

"I'm making ornaments so we can hang something on our Christmas tree when we go to the store and buy it."

"Mr. Nobody, we are going to a special farm to get our tree," explained Mommy. "When I was a young girl and I lived up in Northern British Columbia, we would

12

get into Grandpa's blue and white Ford Truck and drive all the way out of town to the deep pine woods. Grandma would pack Christmas shortbread cookies we baked, mandarin oranges, hot chocolate, and your favorite, coffee!

"We would see a tree out by itself and walk to it through the deep snow. Then we would grab a shovel and dig way down into the cold deep snow and uncover the tree trunk. If the tree met with everyone's approval, Grandpa would cut it down and place the tree into the back of the pick-up truck."

"What happened if you didn't like the tree?" asked Mr. Nobody.

"We would leave the tree and thank him for his time and wish him a Merry Christmas!" Mommy cheekily snickered.

"Ha, ha, Mommy, you're funny. I can't wait till we go to the farm!"

Mr. Nobody and Mommy had fun while we were at school. They tried to make popcorn strings, but Mr. Nobody stuck his big furry paw into the huge bowl and in one swoop, he ate the entire bowl of popcorn. That left only the sour red cranberries.

Next, Mommy tried to do paper chains of pretty red and green paper. But Mr. Nobody got the glue in his long furry brown ears! Mommy then tried paper snowflakes, which worked wonderfully because Mr. Nobody could fold and cut the snowy white paper beautifully!

Finally, the ornaments were ready for the tree. Mommy had to tell Mr. Nobody not to eat any more popcorn, candy canes, or cranberries, and not to touch the colourful glass bulbs!

When we came home from school, we got ready and then off we went to D&D's Family Christmas Tree Farm. There we met Dave and Diane, who ran the farm. Dave gave us a sharp saw and we all ventured off to see the beautiful selection of trees. There were Douglas, Fraser, Grand, and Noble fir, along with Norway and Blue Spruce trees.

We walked all over the property and found a beautiful seven-foot Douglas fir! Mommy held the tree and Daddy cut it down.

"Timber!" We all yelled. The tree gently came down.

Off we trekked to the front, each of taking turns to carrying out the tree. It wasn't heavy like I thought it would be, just difficult to maneuver around the other trees standing in a row!

We went and saw Diane who gave us each a candy cane.

"Candy canes remind us of the shepherds' hook and the 'J' for Jesus!" I exclaimed.

"That's right, Austin!" Daddy beamed.

While drinking our delicious hot chocolate and munching on mini chocolate chip cookies, we sat by the open fire and warmed up a bit. We took our tree home and gave our tree a good drink overnight.

The next day, we placed it in the stand and strung the lights on the tree!

Daddy went to get a cup of coffee, remembering to leave one extra cup out for Mr. Nobody! Mr. Nobody and I started to put the streamers up. First we put up the red and green paper chains, then the popcorn and cranberry string, as well as the foil streamers.

However, Mr. Nobody decided he and I would look much better wrapped up in the foil streamers! Katie came by to help with the tree and decided that maybe she should unravel the two of us before Daddy saw us.

"Oh, you two mischief makers!" Katie giggled. Hope and Page helped Katie unwrap us and then the four of us kids and Mr. Nobody finished placing the beautiful glass bulbs and paper snowflakes on our tree.

Daddy topped the tree with a golden star! The star reminds us that the Star of David shone brightly over the City of Bethlehem the night Jesus was born!

"Mommy, come look at our tree!" called Daddy.

"WOW!" Mommy was proud of us for the great job done on our beautiful Christmas tree!

It was a busy day in the little yellow house. I hope you have fun decorating your house for Christmas!

Love,

Austin

Mr. Nobody and the Miracle of the Christmas Angel!

It was a busy day at the little yellow house. We were getting ready, for tonight was our church Christmas play!

I was going to be one of the wise men, Page was very pleased to be Mary, and Hope was an angel along with Mr. Nobody. Mr. Nobody was so excited to be in the pageant with us that he kept shaking, and hopping up and down. First one foot and then the next foot. Mommy had to tell him to slow down and breathe!

"Deep breaths, in and out through your little black nose, Mr. Nobody!"

Now let me explain something. Mr. Nobody can be seen by children. As for adults, they can only see him if they put their brains into imagination mode. Daddy can see the effects of Mr. Nobody's shenanigans, but sadly Daddy has not seen or met Mr. Nobody.

That night we got all dressed up into our costumes at the church so that we would be all ready for the special night.

Page wore a blue choir gown with a white towel over her head for her part as Mary. I wore a choir gown of red with a gold cape and a gold crown. Mr. Nobody and Hope wore paper wings that sparkled, a silver tinsel garland, and a white choir gown and they carried a long sparkler.

When Mr. Nobody saw my long red gown, gold cape, and gold crown, he was in awe as to how majestic I looked!

"Why are you so fancy shmancy, Austin?"

"Well, I'm representing one of the wise men that came to see Jesus when He was born."

"Wasn't there three wise guys?" Mr. Nobody asked.

"You mean, three wise men," replied Hope. "These wise men travelled from foreign lands following the Star of David that shone brightly in the sky! We don't know what countries but, the Bible says From the East. That is why we sing the song, *We Three Kings of Orient Are* in this play."

"I wonder who wrote the song?" I asked Hope and Page.

"Well Austin, it was written by John Henry Hopkin in 1857," proclaimed Mrs. Jones, our music pastor.

"Why did they bring gold, frankincense and myrrh?" I asked Mrs. Jones.

"Well, gold was used to symbolise a gold crown, for Jesus is the King."

"Just like in the song!" we all chimed!

gold   frankincense   myrrh

Mrs. Jones went on to explain frankincense was used to praise Jesus and was also very expensive. Only royalty could afford to buy frankincense. And sadly, the myrrh was used to preserve the body in death.

"We better get our sparklers and line up, Hope. It's time for the pageant to begin!" Mr. Nobody was sooo excited!

We all lined up in pageant order. Mary, followed by the wise men, followed by the shepherds and the angels. The sparklers were lit. Hope was a bit nervous, because the sparklers spit and sputtered out real flames of fire.

We all started to walk, then Mrs. Jones noticed that we were going too fast so she told us to stop. Mr. Nobody was not paying attention to his sparkler.

Do you know what happened? Mr. Nobody accidently lit Hope's angel wing on fire! Mr. Nobody started to walk with the rest of the group of children when Mrs. Cougar noticed that Hope's angel wings were on fire!

Mrs. Cougar got out of the pew and stopped Mr. Nobody and the rest of the children from going further.

Hope had no idea that her wings were on fire. Daddy and Mommy were in the second pew, but there were too many people sitting in the pew beside them for Daddy to get to Hope!

As Hope went up the stairs to the front of the church, the other children were astonished and started to back away from her. Mr. Nobody saw that Hope's wing was on fire and shouted, "Oh no!"

But with the organ playing and all the children singing, let alone all the commotion of people scurrying up to help keep Hope safe, Hope only heard the "Oh no!" and "Oohs" from the audience.

"Did I do that with my sparkler?" Mr. Nobody started to cry. He realized that now Hope was in real danger!

"It's okay, Mr. Nobody!" the other kids comforted Mr. Nobody and eventually he stopped crying and started praying in his heart for Hope to be safe. She did not have a clue what was happening! Hope was surprised and confused. *What was happening?* she thought. Why were people turning away from her? Did she smell funny? Did she look really special? Hope turned and looked over her right shoulder and saw a tiny bit of the flames just as Mr. York extinguished the fire.

"What happened? What's going on?" Hope started to cry.

Mr. York gave Hope a hug and gently told her that her wings had been on fire but she was safe now.

"Thank you, Mr. York!" Hope replied shyly.

The rest of the children and Mr. Nobody came up on stage singing "We Three Kings of Orient Are." Then Mr. York and everyone went back to their seats. The other children were singing and the beautiful church filled with joy, peace, and much rejoicing!

Mr. Nobody placed his big furry paw on Hope's shoulder. Hope kept singing and shook her head at Mr. Nobody!

Page and I realized we witnessed a miracle that night!

As the wise men sang with the shepherds, angels, Joseph, and Mary, we were so thankful for the love of community to save a little girl's life and to have the freedom to worship Jesus.

After we had performed, we went to the church basement for Christmas cookies and hot cocoa.

Hope was happy, but a bit overwhelmed by all the attention! Mr. Nobody apologised to Hope and Hope reciprocated with a big mushy kiss! Thank goodness Mr. Nobody likes hugs and goopy kisses!

I don't like kisses from my sisters, but that night I think I would have endured a kiss just because I was so glad to know my sister Hope was safe.

It was a busy little yellow house filled with love and relief that night.

Remember to watch what you are doing, especially around fire!

Keep safe always.

Love,

Austin

Mr. Nobody's Shenanigans on Christmas Day!

It was an exciting day at our little yellow house, because it was Christmas Day!

I woke up at 6:00 in the morning. The sun was not even up, it was so dark outside! Mr. Nobody was snoring away and his big brown and white furry toes were wiggling. Mr. Nobody was dreaming!

I wonder what he was dreaming. Can you guess?

I heard someone in the bathroom, so I quietly got out of bed and waited just beside the door. When the door opened I yelled, "BOO! MERRY CHRISTMAS!"

Good thing Mommy had just gone to the bathroom, otherwise I think she would have peed herself! Mommy jumped up and screamed "AHHHH! What on Earth!" Mommy patted her chest and took a deep breath. "Merry Christmas to you, too, Austin. Ya scared me!"

"I know, you jumped and screamed, " I chuckled.

"I suppose you want to open your stocking and your gifts, too? Well, you might want to get your sisters up. I'll put the coffee on and that will get Daddy and Mr. Nobody up for sure!"

"Daddy, wake up! Let's get this show on the road!" Mommy shouted at Daddy, but it was no use.

"It's too early! It's a holiday, I'm too sleepy!" complained Daddy.

I raced downstairs and jumped on top of Hope and Page who were cuddled up together in the same bed. "Merry Christmas!" I hollered. "Come on, Mommy said we can open stockings and gifts! Let's go!"

"What, what, we can?" my sisters sputtered. The twins got up and put on some slippers and sweaters sleepily, and slowly dragged themselves up the stairs to the living room.

As for Katie, she would not move. I turned on her lights, I pulled off the bed covers, and I bravely jumped on top of her (I say bravely jumped 'cause she is a teenager who could get really mad at me and then I'm dead). So, I ran upstairs and got something hard and very cold!

Can you guess what it was? Yup, you're right! It was an ice pack! I ran downstairs and quickly put the ice pack on Katie's warm tummy. Then I ran and hid under the couch to avoid the raging teenager I had just created!

Katie streaked up the stairs and ran right into something. "What, I can't see... who's got me—" SMACK!!! Katie got kissed. But by who?

Mr. Nobody was under the mistletoe, invisible! He was hiding and waiting to kiss someone under the mistletoe! "MERRY CHRISTMAS, KATIE!"

Poor Katie. She sputtered Mr. Nobody's fur out of her mouth and then stumbled to the couch and plunked herself down! I quietly sneaked out from under the couch, than I noticed that something was missing...make that two somethings that were missing.

The stockings were gone. "Mr. Nobody, where are the stockings?" I pleaded. Daddy poured two cups of coffee, one for him and one for Mr. Nobody. Then, he noticed there was a streak of crumbs leading out to the garage.

"The gingerbread house! Where did the gingerbread house go?" We four kids shrieked.

"Mr. Nobody, what did you do now?" pleaded Mommy.

"I found the stockings in the recycle bins. Luckily they are perfectly fine!" I shouted. "As for the trail of crumbs, that looks like something Mr. Nobody ate!"

"Oops, sorry!" Mr. Nobody said. "I couldn't resist hiding the stockings and eating the delicious gingerbread house."

"Mr. Nobody, try and behave yourself today, okay? Here, open your stocking." Mommy sighed.

"Now we can't eat the ginger bread house we made!" Hope sulked

"Oh, but you can, because I hid an extra gingerbread house under the Christmas tree!" Mommy chuckled.

"That's a good idea to have a backup plan!" Page giggled.

After a quick breakfast, we opened our brightly coloured paper-wrapped gifts.

Mr. Nobody played a great practical joke on Page.

"Here is a tag with Page's name on it," Daddy noticed. "Say what! Let's follow the clues and see where it leads to. First clue: Makes my favorite drink?"

"Coffee!" Page laughed and looked at the coffee machine. "Next clue...What has white flowers and hangs?"

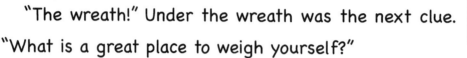

"The wreath!" Under the wreath was the next clue. "What is a great place to weigh yourself?"

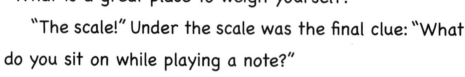

"The scale!" Under the scale was the final clue: "What do you sit on while playing a note?"

"Now that's a tough one," I wondered.

"The piano, you sit on the bench!"

Sure enough, inside the piano bench was Page's gift! It was a music CD she really wanted. Page started dancing all over the house and yelling at the top of her voice. "I love it! Yeah! Can't wait to dance!"

We laughed at Page as she shook and twisted herself all over the entire living room!

"Now for Mr. Nobody's final gift!" Page announced.

Mr. Nobody opened a shiny gold box to find a beautiful tree ornament. It was a little wooden manger scene of Mary, Joseph, and baby Jesus with a gallantly painted Star of David!

"To remind you that Jesus is the reason for the season and not just for shenanigans!" Mommy exclaimed.

Mr. Nobody hung the ornament up on the tree near the top for us all to see. With the radio playing *Silent Night,* we knew who the greatest gift was...JESUS!

It was a busy house that day. So full of love, peace, and hope, for the future and for always!

Merry Christmas!

With Love,
Daddy, Mommy, Katie, Hope,
Page, Austin, and Mr. Nobody!

CPSIA information can be obtained
at www.ICGtesting.com
Printed in the USA
450087LV00001B/1

9 781486 605729